James Christopher Carroll

MOTHER WINTER

Creative Ⓒ Editions

If you are awake,
on the longest cold night,
when the wind curls and frost holds time,
you'll hear her bells and smell the first snow,
when Mother Winter goes walking.

Go out and find her,
she's waiting for you,
go and ride on her long coattails,
wander this eve, dark and deep,
when Mother Winter goes walking.

Through the town,
past windows so warm,
into woods,
trees bending hello,
across the field,
so quickly we glide,
while rabbits and possums and chickadees chase,
when Mother Winter goes walking.

Cross pond ice,
where fishies still bubble below,
in and out of shadows,
silently alive,
over hills blessed,
blue against the sky,

while the stars rise, loving eyes above it all,
when Mother Winter goes walking.

Climbing higher,
white drifts about us now,
covering caps and mittens and boots,
we are all snowballs,
and snowboys,

snowgirls and snowangels,
with frost about our faces,
and each breath a frozen wreath around our heads,
when Mother Winter goes walking.

So, if you are awake,
on the longest cold night,
when the wind curls and frost holds time,

you'll hear her bells and smell the first snow,
when Mother Winter goes walking.

In a night kissed with quiet color,
she wanders a world already dreaming.

Go out and find her.

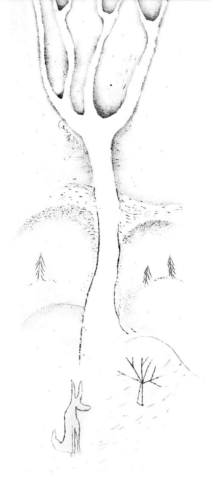

Text and illustrations copyright © 2022 by James Christopher Carroll

Edited by Kate Riggs and Amy Novesky / Designed by Rita Marshall

Published in 2022 by Creative Editions / P. O. Box 227, Mankato, MN 56002 USA

Creative Editions is an imprint of The Creative Company / www.thecreativecompany.us

Library of Congress Cataloging-in-Publication Data

Names: Carroll, James Christopher, 1960- author, illustrator.

Title: Mother Winter / James Christopher Carroll.

Summary: A poetic personification of the winter season, Mother Winter goes
walking "on the longest cold night," inviting the reader along to experience
chill winds, icy ponds, white snowdrifts, and other quiet wonders.

Identifiers: LCCN 2021034150 / ISBN 9781568463773 (hardcover)

ISBN 9781682770900 (paperback)

Subjects: LCSH: Children's poetry, American. / CYAC: Winter—Poetry. / LCGFT: Poetry.

Classification: LCC PS3603.A774577 M68 2022 (print)

DDC 811/.6—dc23/eng/20211018

LC record available at https://lccn.loc.gov/2021034150

First edition 9 8 7 6 5 4 3 2 1

JAN - - 2023